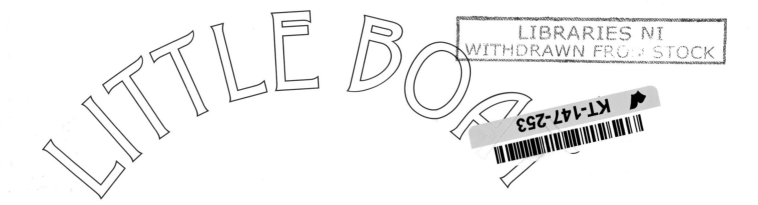

LITTLE BOAT

templar publishing

The ocean is a **big** place and I am just a little boat.

But I chart my own course

and I drop my own anchor.

The sea is always changing and full of dangers,

but I sail on…

through terrible storms,

up and down

rolling waves...

past **giant** sea monsters…

in search of . . .

Together, we dive down to the bottom.

and climb up to the top.

We go round and round in circles...

and never want to stop.

Full steam ahead to the edge of the world...

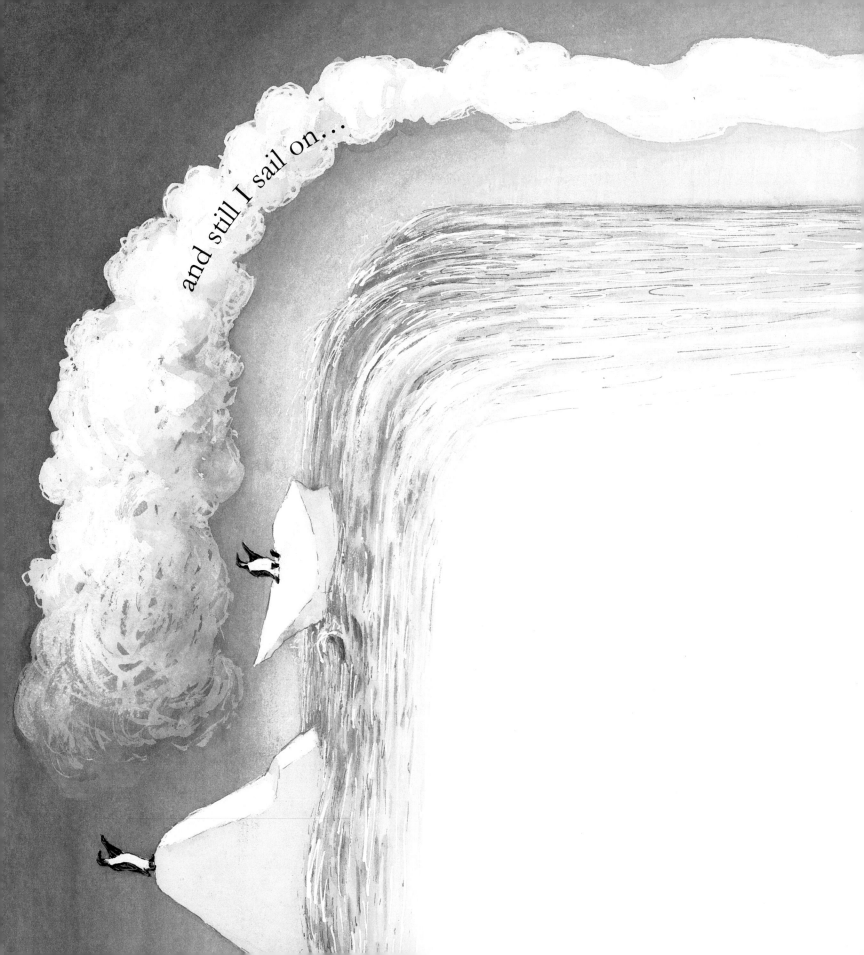

and still I sail on...

because now no ocean is too big…

for a little boat like me.

 – T. D.

A TEMPLAR BOOK

First published in the UK in hardback in 2008 by Templar Publishing
This softback edition published in 2009 by Templar Publishing,
an imprint of The Templar Company Limited,
Deepdene Lodge, Deepdene Avenue, Dorking, Surrey, RH5 4AT, UK
www.templarco.co.uk

Copyright © 2008 by Thomas Docherty

10 9 8 7 6 5 4

ISBN 978-1-84011-836-0

Printed in Hong Kong